Authors note.

The whole idea for this book, was to encourage children, especially of primary school ages, to pick up a book, that contained text that they would want to read. With no pressure from school, parent or society. The readable words and the tongue in cheek humour, which seems just a little bit silly and a little bit naughty, appealed so much to my 6 year old, that it inspired him to create scenes all by himself, which ended up in this book.

One day, before Ryan could speak properly, he overheard his parents describe the worst smell in his life, as farts. He did not like it at all. He disliked them so much that he cried whenever he smelled farts and so he decided that he would never ever fart, ever!

One day, as Ryan and his dad looked through photos of Ryan's birthday party, they both noticed how close to daddy's head, the size of Ryan's own head was. Ryan was 5 years old
Ryan had heard that your brain made you clever so he asked daddy. "Does my big head mean that I have got a big and clever brain, Daddy?"

"Oh yes son! You certainly have got daddy's brains!" Dad exclaimed. Ryan was very happy.

As Ryan and his dad looked through photos of his 6th birthday party, Ryan noticed that his head was the same size as his dads! Ryan said to his dad.
"I am cleverer than you daddy, because I am younger and have a bigger brain, ain't I Daddy?"

Dad looked at Ryan in confusion and as Ryan looked so expectant, he answered.
"Of course son! You are the cleverest son in the whole wide world!"

Ryan and his mum, looked through his 8th birthday party photos.
Mum said, "Ryan, we need to go to the emergency at once!"

Ryan looked at mum, shook his massive head, which by now barely fit through the living room door, sadly.
Mum just did not understand that my brain was growing with me.

He followed her to the doctor,
who was just around the corner
The doctor took out his stethoscope and other interesting stuff

He checked Ryan out all the way through and came to a decision.
He asked Ryan and his mum to take a seat with him.
He told them gently, that every night whilst Ryan slept,
his farts 3 by 3 had been gong into his head!

Ryan told him that he was telling a lie and that he was only jealous!

Ryan's mum was very worried indeed but took off after Ryan so he would get home safe
and not roll down the road.

Alas, Ryan's head got as big as the house and sadly mum and dad wedged him in.

"Ryan, we love you and would always do, but our darling son, you need to let out your farts" they said gently.

"3 by 3 the doctor said and more if you could, yet no more than 20 a day. For although you have to let out over 1000 a year, more than 20 might be quite smelly and may knock you and others out! They said to Ryan.

Ryan looked on sadly. At their loving but silly not understanding faces.
He looked at the house that he could no longer fit into.
Looked at his mum and dad's faces, very slowly rumbled to his feet and started to run, run away from it all.

As he run, his head begun to get bigger and bigger and bigger! His tiny legs you could not see as his head got bigger than the town!

He run faster than he had ever run and could ever run.

In fear and desperation, his mum called out "RYAN!!!" So loudly, that it somehow got through to Ryan!

Upon hearing his name, Ryan swung round, lost his balance and ... people got out of the way! Cars got out of the way! Aeroplanes got out of the way!

Then as in slow motion, peoples faces went from fear to interest as Ryan's head hit the ground! AND

WHOOOOOOOOOOOOOOOOOOOOOOOOOOOSH!

he most almighty windy pop,
rushed out and swept the whole of the people, the sea, the fishes and animals out of Europe.

The next day, in Africa, there were double the people and they were so much more rich!

This book is dedicated to ;
Ethan David Potts
Stacie Prempeh
Elsie Prempeh
Daisy Prempeh

This book is the first of our two part book.
In the second part, Ryan's adventures take on the most incredible twist, in Africa. The results would shake the very foundations of the enitre earth!

Finally, a big thank you to all our cheeky little friends, who inspired us to put our thoughts and imagination unto paper and print.

Printed in Great Britain
by Amazon